The Happiest Tree
A YOGA STORY

BY Uma Krishnaswami
ILLUSTRATIONS BY Ruth Jeyaveeran

LEE & LOW BOOKS INC. • NEW YORK

doh (though): two
ek (ake): one
gup-choop (gup-choop): silent, dumbstruck
matthi (mutt-hee): crumbly snack usually made with flour, salt, spices, and butter or oil
na (nah): no
rani (rah-nee): queen; also used as a term of endearment
yoga (yoh-guh): ancient Indian system of meditation and exercise

Thanks to Debbie McMurray for her help with Auntie's yoga instructions to her class.   U.K.

Text copyright © 2005 by Uma Krishnaswami
Illustrations copyright © 2005 by Ruth Jeyaveeran

LEE & LOW BOOKS Inc.
95 Madison Avenue, New York, NY 10016
leeandlow.com

Manufactured in China

Book design by Tania Garcia
Book production by The Kids at Our House

The text is set in Baskerville
The illustrations are rendered in acrylic

10 9 8 7 6 5 4 3 2 1
First Edition

Library of Congress Cataloging-in-Publication Data
Krishnaswami, Uma.
   The happiest tree : a yoga story / by Uma Krishnaswami ; illustrations by Ruth Jeyaveeran.—1st ed.
      p. cm.
   Summary: Embarrassed by her clumsiness, eight-year-old Meena, an Asian Indian American girl, is reluctant to appear in the school play until she gains self-confidence by practicing yoga.
   ISBN 1-58430-237-2
[1. Yoga—Fiction. 2. Self-confidence—Fiction. 3. Theater—Fiction. 4. East Indian Americans—Fiction.] I. Jeyaveeran, Ruth, ill. II. Title.
PZ7.K8978Ha 2005
[E]—dc22   2004027851
ISBN-13: 978-1-58430-237-7

For Sally Davies—U.K.

For my family—R.J.

Meena was excited about the play her class was writing—
a new and improved version of *Red Riding Hood*. She laughed
out loud when they decided that Grandma would chase the
wolf. She liked figuring out how the story would end for
the woodcutter. And she loved painting the sets . . . until she
spilled the paint.

"It's okay," said Meena's teacher, Mrs. Jackson. But Meena
felt terrible.

When the class chose parts, Meena pretended she wasn't interested.

"Meena, everyone gets to play a part," said Mrs. Jackson.

Meena shook her head. All she could say was "I can't. I'm too clumsy."

Mrs. Jackson would not take no for an answer. "Of course you can," she said. "You can be a tree. We need lots of trees in the forest."

Soon it was time for the first rehearsal. Walking onto the stage, Meena hoped she wouldn't stumble. She hoped she wouldn't trip.

But then she stumbled. She tripped. She almost fell.

"Meeee-na . . . ," groaned the other trees.

Meena wished she could fall right through the stage and become a disappearing tree.

At dinner that night Meena drooped. "I'm the worst tree in the world," she said.

"Why?" asked Mom. "What happened?"

Meena told her parents about the rehearsal and how she had tripped and stumbled.

"It's all right, Meena *rani*," said Mom. "It's just that your arms and legs are growing really fast. That can make you feel clumsy sometimes."

"You don't have to be perfect," Dad added. "Just try your best."

"I'm perfectly clumsy," Meena said sadly.

The next day Meena and her mother went to the Indian grocery store to buy rice and flour and spices. There was so much to see! Meena whirled around, looking.

"Careful," cautioned Mom.

"I'm being careful," said Meena. She leaned forward to look at a little brass bell. A bag of rice toppled over.

"It's all right," said Mrs. Vohra, the owner of the store. "Let her look." She gave Meena a piece of *matthi* to munch on. The spicy flavors of the crumbly snack danced in Meena's mouth.

"Thank you, Auntie," said Meena. Mrs. Vohra was everyone's auntie.

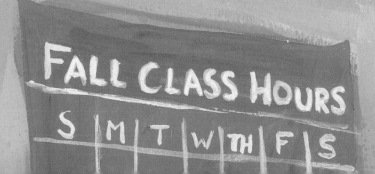

NEW YOGA FOR KIDS

Suddenly Meena saw something that made her fall *gup-choop* silent in astonishment. Through a window in the back of the store, in the room beyond, she saw feet! They rose up into the air. They stayed very still. Then slowly they went back down.

"That's one of our yoga classes," said Auntie. "Would you like to join my children's class?"

"I'm too clumsy," said Meena.

"Clumsy shumsy," said Auntie. "Just try it and see, *na*?"

Meena watched the window. Now hands rose up in the air. Meena raised her own arms. She joined her palms over her head.

"Oh my," Auntie said. "You're doing better already." So Meena agreed to sign up for yoga class.

umbai
llah

Anil Kapoor

FALL CLASS HOURS

S	M	T	W	TH	F	S

Yoga class was not easy, but Meena tried her best. She breathed slowly and deeply. She stretched like a rubber band.

"Let's do the cat pose," said Auntie. "Breathe in. Arch up . . . breathe out. Down . . . breathe in."

Meena breathed in and out and arched her back up and down, but then she lost her balance. Her foot shot out and she nearly hit the yoga cat behind her.

"Now the frog pose," said Auntie. "Down on your knees. . . . Sit back on your feet. . . . Knees wide open. . . . Bend your body forward."

Meena bent her body low, but when she tried to put her hands on the floor to rest on her lily pad, she fell over.

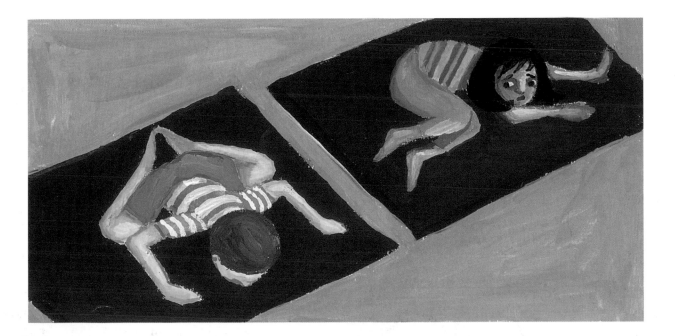

Meena stretched and breathed her way through yoga class.
Auntie told her what she did correctly, and helped her with
the difficult parts. Soon Meena could breathe deeply and make
herself still. Her feet didn't shoot out so much. She didn't topple
over as often.

"Very nice, Meena," said Auntie.

Meena felt golden warm inside.

During rehearsals for *Red Riding Hood*, Meena tried to be
still and quiet, but her feet had trouble staying rooted. She kept
looking around. She laughed at all the funny parts. She wanted
to say the lines when her classmates forgot them.

"Meena, stay still," said one of the other trees.

"Only your branches are supposed to move," said another.

"Shhh," said a third.

Meena tried her best, but it was hard keeping her arms and
legs from moving around.

In yoga class, though, Meena's
arms and legs learned to work in
smooth, slow movements. She
stretched out flat on her stomach
and kept her feet together. Then
she propped herself up on her
arms and raised her head, turning
left, then right, in the cobra pose.

One day Auntie announced,
"We're going to try the tree pose."

"Oh no!" cried Meena. "I'm a
terrible tree."

Auntie looked puzzled, so Meena
explained about the class play.

"I understand," Auntie said.
"But a yoga tree is different. Just
take a deep breath. Hold it for two
seconds . . . *ek, doh* . . . and let it go."

Meena began to relax. She
rooted her feet and raised her
arms. She breathed and breathed.
She calmed down. Her worries
went away.

After a few weeks Meena found it easy to breathe slowly and deeply in yoga class.

One day when all the children were sitting in the lotus pose, a thought lit up in Meena's mind. *I can change my body by how I feel inside,* she realized. *If I am quiet inside, my body will be still. That's what yoga is really about.*

Meena hugged her thought to herself. It filled her with gladness. She imagined herself standing tall and still, growing roots in Red Riding Hood's forest.

On the night of the performance of the new and improved version of *Red Riding Hood,* Mom and Dad drove Meena to school.

Meena and her classmates put on their costumes. Meena's sweatshirt and tights were stretchy and soft, but her tree branches tickled and her roots scratched.

"Don't worry, Meena *rani,*" said Mom. "You'll be fine."

"We know you'll be a great tree," said Dad.

"Onstage everyone," Mrs. Jackson announced. "It's time to start the play."

That was when it happened. As Meena walked onto the stage, one of her branches snagged Red Riding Hood's cloak. Then Meena's right foot stepped on the roots of her left foot.

She tripped. She almost fell down.

"Meena!" whispered the other trees.

"Meena, leave your broken roots behind," said Mrs. Jackson. "Just do the best you can."

Meena kicked her way out of the pile of roots.
She looked around for a place to hide. How could
she be a tree without her roots?

Through the curtains, Meena saw the audience gathering.
She found Mom and Dad. She spotted someone else too.
Auntie had come to see Meena be a tree.

Meena knew she couldn't hide, so she started her yoga breathing. In . . . out. In . . . out. She got so quiet she could feel her heart beating. Then she stood up straight in her best tall tree way, raised her arms high, and took her place onstage.

Never mind those silly old roots! Meena thought. She would grow her own yoga tree roots, right into the floor of the forest.

The curtains opened and the play went on. Grandma chased away the wolf. The woodcutter became a recycled paper salesman. And Red Riding Hood wrote a play about her scary day in the forest.

Through it all Meena took deep breaths and let them out. She was still when she needed to be still. She moved slowly and carefully when she needed to move. Best of all, she knew she could do this again, anytime she wanted to.

Meena was the happiest tree in the whole forest.

More About Yoga

Yoga, or hatha yoga, has been practiced in India for many centuries. Today it is popular all over the world.

Yoga is a way of learning to become aware of your body and your mind and how they work together. People who practice yoga learn to breathe deeply. They begin to recognize the way their bodies move, and to control and balance their movements. At the same time they learn to focus on the present moment and calm their minds.

Here are the yoga poses Meena learned in the story.

Tree

Frog

Lotus

Cat

Cobra

Yoga Books for Children

Lark, Liz. *Yoga for Kids*. Richmond Hill, Ontario: Firefly, 2003.

Pegrum, Juliet. *Kid Yoga: Fun with a Twist*. New York: Sterling, 2004.

Stewart, Mary, and Kathy Phillips. *Yoga for Children*. New York: Fireside, 1992.